ship shapes

Written by Stella Blackstone   Illustrated by Siobhan Bell

 Barefoot Books
step inside a story

All aboard! Come along with me!
Let's see what shapes we can find on the sea.

Square

Circle

Triangle

Star

Rectangle

Semi-circle

Diamond

Crescent

Oval

Can you count all of these triangles?

What are the shapes
of these sails?

What can you see on this steamboat?

And on this wild sea monster's tail?

What are the shapes
of these small fish?

What shape is this green submarine?

And this treasure that twinkles and gleams?

Now that our voyage is over,
It's time to sail quietly home.

And count up the shapes we've been shown.

For my mother, with much love — Stella Blackstone
For Maureen Guilfoyle — Siobhan Bell

Barefoot Books, 294 Banbury Road, Oxford, OX2 7ED

Barefoot Books, 2067 Massachusetts Ave, Cambridge, MA 02140

First published in Great Britain by Barefoot Books, Ltd
and in the United States of America by Barefoot Books, Inc in 2006
The paperback edition first published in 2012

Graphic design by Judy Linard, London
Reproduction by Grafiscan, Verona
Printed in China on 100% acid-free paper
This book was typeset in Carrotflower Regular
The illustrations were prepared using hand-dyed cotton sheets

Board book ISBN 978-1-84686-157-4
Paperback ISBN 978-1-84686-762-0

British Cataloguing-in-Publication Data:
a catalogue record for this book is available from the British Library
Library of Congress Cataloging-in-Publication Data
is available under LCCN 2005019937

3 5 7 9 8 6 4 2